Tibs
The Post Office Cat

By Joyce Dunbar
Illustrated by Claire Fletcher

words & pictures

Text copyright © 2017 Joyce Dunbar

Illustrations copyright © 2017 Claire Fletcher

First published in 2017 by words & pictures
Part of The Quarto Group
The Old Brewery, 6 Blundell Street, London, N7 9BH

A catalogue record for this book is available from the British Library.

ISBN 978 1 91027 720 1

1 3 5 7 9 8 6 4 2

Printed in China

Dear Reader,

This story is about a cat called Tibs. Tibs was a real cat. He was born in a Post Office in November 1950. It was Tibs' job to keep all the mice and rats under control. He even got paid! Two shillings and sixpence a week, which was enough to buy him some delicious milk. He did such a good job that they named him "Tibs the Great".

The Post Office staff in those days liked to have parties on special occasions – with Tibs as guest of honour. Sometimes they had parties deep underground. This was because the Royal Mail had a very special train called the Mail Rail. This was an electric train that travelled under the streets of London. It didn't have a driver but happily trundled along delivering mail from Whitechapel to Paddington – sometimes it delivered four million letters in a day! Not many people knew about it. Tibs loved his job and had lots of fun.

We hope you enjoy his story.

The Head Postmaster

There was trouble at the Sorting Office in Mount Pleasant.

Holes in the mail sacks!
Letters torn to shreds!
Stamps licked through to the glue!

The Post Office sorters scratched their heads. "We can't deliver these!" they complained. "There's only half an address. And no stamp!"

Who or what was to blame?

MICE, of course!

The head postmaster called a meeting.
"This is serious. We need a cat. A proper mouser.
We've got a big event coming up and everything
has to be perfect!"

"What about Minnie's kitten?" suggested the
cook. "She was a great mouser and her kitten
might be old enough now."

In a small Post Office, where he lived with his mother Minnie, a white-whiskered cat called Tibs was relaxing.

Christmas had been and gone, with its tinsel, trimmings and toys; then Valentine's Day with its red hearts and roses; and now it was Easter, with its feathery chicks and fluffy bunnies − one celebration fading into another.

"Come here, Tibs," called his mother. "Today we have something special to celebrate. You know that you are Tibs, son of Toodle, son of Tiddles, son of Toby. You come from a long line of distinguished career cats."

"What's a career?" asked Tibs.

"It's a very important job. Tomorrow you are going to the Central Sorting Office. You will be chief mouser!"

"But I like it here," Tibs said.

"Nonsense," said his mother, and she gave him the grooming of his life so that he would look his best.

The next day, Tibs arrived at the busy sorting office. He sat on a chair in front of the head postmaster's desk.

"Mmmmm," said the postmaster. "You look the part. We will hire you for a trial period."

"It is your job to keep the building free of mice," he said. "You will be paid two shillings and sixpence a week and as many mice as you can catch."

Tibs felt a little worried. As a young kitten, one of his best friends had been a mouse. His name was Fred. They had played games of hide-and-seek and 'What's the time, Mr Tibs?'

But now he was in the big wide world and he had responsibilities...

Watching and listening all the while
from his hiding place was a mouse.
He scurried back to tell the other mice.

FOOD TAKEN FROM THE
CANTEEN MUST NOT
BE CONSUMED IN
THE LOUNGE AREAS.

"He looks really fierce, with flaring
white whiskers and sharp claws. We'd
better watch out," he warned.

That evening, Tibs wandered around the Sorting Office. It was a huge, echoey building.

Tibs felt homesick.

He longed for his mother and the small Post Office he had come from, where everyone knew everybody's name. He longed for the queues and the chatter and the 'thank yous' and 'hellos' and 'how are yous'.

But then, Tibs found his way into the basement kitchen where there was a big scrap bin...

...and some left-over butter! He suddenly felt much better.
Tibs was busy licking butter from his paws when a dollop
dropped onto the floor.

For one little mouse, the temptation was too much.

He crept closer...

and closer...

until...

Tibs did what any polite, well-brought
up cat would do.

"Hello," he said. "My name's Tibs.
What's yours?"

The mouse froze. He'd never met a cat like this.

"I don't have a name," he muttered.

"Don't you?" said Tibs. "You look like a Fred to me!"

"Fred?" said the delighted mouse.
"I like that name!"

Suddenly, the mice came creeping out from their holes and hiding places.

"What's my name?" asked one of the mice.
"What's mine?" they all squeaked.

Tibs didn't know what to call them.
He needed time to think. So he stretched and yawned, until the mice had quietened down.

When they were silent, Tibs began, "I am Tibs, son of Toodle, son of Tiddles, son of Toby. I am also a trusted employee of the Post Office. If you want names, I think you'll have to earn them."

"How do we do that?" asked Fred.
"You need some proper training," said Tibs.

With that, he ordered the mice back to the sorting room to find a letter each. This time, instead of nibbling the letters, they tried to walk on their hind legs, balancing the letters on their noses.

The mice tottered and teetered about, but soon got the hang of it.

They sorted the letters neatly, ready for the Post Office workers the next day.

Tibs rewarded them with the best left-overs from the scrap bin, which were much tastier than the letters.

And the scraps he chose for himself were much tastier than mice!

As the weeks passed, the mice became very good at their new job. Tibs soon found another task for them to do: polishing the shillings he was paid each week!

The mice were so eager to have names that they learnt all sorts of things.

How to tidy up the pencils...

sweep the floor...

walk in line...

scoop poop...

...and above all, how to
keep out of sight!

The head postmaster was delighted. "Thanks to Tibs, the building is clear of mice. It's spotless! Now we can make plans for the Coronation party!" he exclaimed.

Everyone was excited that Princess Elizabeth was going to be crowned Queen. It was all anybody could talk about!

The Royal Mail, as her Majesty's Service, was planning a special celebration. All the families of the Post Office employees would attend as well as the children from the orphanage.

"Now, there's lots to organize," he announced. "The party will take place on the platform of the underground Mail Rail and all the children will be given a ride. For an extra treat, three of our loyal members of staff have volunteered as entertainers. Please give a cheer for our clown, magician and fiddler."

Just before the party, Tibs was taken down to the Mail Rail station and put on special duty.

"More work for you, Mr Tibs," said the postmaster. "We need you to patrol the area and guard the presents."

"Oh glory!" thought Tibs.

As soon as the coast was clear, Tibs called to the mice for help. "All aboard! Single file. Tails tucked in. No messing!"

But they had unexpected company...

In the distance, a few carriages along,
were three very strange people...

"Robbers," whispered Tibs. "Robbers in disguise!
Trying to steal the children's presents, I'll bet.
Come on Fred. Lead the charge."

The mice jumped on the robbers. They ran up their sleeves and down their trousers, before putting mail sacks over their heads and tying them up!

This was surely enough to win them names?

Finally it was time for the party. The children bustled in excitement as they waited in line to be given a name badge. Then the train arrived with Tibs on top!

But what was behind him? It looked like three bulging sacks, wriggling and squirming. The head postmaster looked very worried. Were they full of the mice Tibs had caught?

They soon found out. Emerging sheepish and dazed from the sacks was the cook, dressed as a clown, the sub-postmaster, in his magician's outfit and the fiddler with his fiddle – all with very red faces!

They muttered something about hijacking mice, but everyone was far too excited to listen. "Ha ha!" laughed the head postmaster. "What a stunt! Great entertainment. Well done, everybody!"

What a party they had! Tibs was declared
'the cream of the cats', and had his photograph
taken for the Post Office Magazine.

Best of all, he was given a special collar with
a medal engraved with the letters H.M.P.O.C.
They stood for 'Her Majesty's Post Office Cat'.

Finally, everybody went home.
But all was not done.

The mice had been promised a
reward and were waiting eagerly.

"We want our names!" they chanted.

Tibs was a clever cat but he still couldn't think of any more mouse names and he couldn't call them all Fred.

Just in time, he remembered that the children had been given name tags at the party – and had left them all in the postmaster's hat on the way out.

"Here," said Tibs, offering the hat. "A lucky dip. Now don't all rush together. One at a time."

"I'm Melvyn,"
squeaked one delighted mouse.

"I'm Edwina," squeaked another.

"And I am Tibs, son of Toodle,
son of Tiddles, son of Toby...

...I am the Post Office Cat!"